Do You See
MY TAIL?

Clavis
NEW YORK

Anita Bijsterbosch

Do you see my tail?
I have a soft, bushy tail.
Guess who I am!

Hello, squirrel.
Hello, sweet baby squirrels.

That's right, I'm a squirrel!
My babies live in a nest in a hollow tree.
They like acorns.

**Do you see my tail?
I have a cute little tail.
Guess who I am!**

Hello, deer.
Hello, sweet baby deer.

Well done! I am a deer!
My baby is lying in a little nest in the high grass.
She loves giving kisses.

Do you see my tail?
I have a long tail with feathers.
Guess who I am!

Hello, bird.
Hello, sweet baby birds.

Yes, I am a bird!
My babies are sitting in a nest in the tree.
How loudly they chirp!

Do you see my tail?
I have a big, flat tail.
Guess who I am!

Hello, rabbit.
Hello, sweet baby rabbits.

Good guess! I am a rabbit! My babies are hopping around in a hole under the ground. They want to play all day long.

Do you see my tail?
I have a bushy tail
that comes to a point.
Guess who I am!

Hello, fox.
Hello, sweet baby foxes.

That's right. I am a fox!
My babies are playing in a nest under the ground.
They love to frolic.

**Do you see my tail?
I have a teeny tiny tail.
Guess who I am!**

Hello, hedgehog.
Hello, sweet baby hedgehogs.

Yes! I am a hedgehog! My babies
are sleeping and eating in a nest
made of branches and leaves.
They love apples.

First published in Belgium and Holland by Clavis Uitgeverij, Hasselt – Amsterdam, 2016
Copyright © 2016, Clavis Uitgeverij

English translation from the Dutch by Clavis Publishing Inc. New York
Copyright © 2017 for the English language edition: Clavis Publishing Inc. New York

Visit us on the web at www.clavisbooks.com

Do You See My Tail? written and illustrated by Anita Bijsterbosch
Original title: *Zie je mjin staart?*
Translated from the Dutch by Clavis Publishing

ISBN 978-1-60537-320-1

This book was printed in July 2016 at CP Printing (Heyuan) Limited,
Heyuan Hi-Tech Development Zone, Heyuan, Guangdong Province,
P.R.C. Postal Code: 517000, China

First Edition
10 9 8 7 6 5 4 3 2 1